The Vampire
Who Had No Fangs

Written and Illustrated
by Duane Porter

Buried Treasure Publishing

ISBN 978-0-9800993-7-9

ISBN 09800993-7-4

Published by
Buried Treasure Publishing
Blue Springs, Missouri

BuriedTreasurePublishing.com

Printed in the U.S.A.

for Olivia

Olivia wasn't like the other little vampire kids.

While they had fun sneaking out every night to drink the blood from rabbits or foxes or cattle for their midnight snacks, Olivia had to hang around the castle.

You see, Olivia had no fangs.

Having no fangs is a problem if you're a vampire. Vampires are supposed to have two long, sharp fangs right where normal humans like us have our sharp pointy teeth called incisors.

They use them to bite the necks of their victims, making two little holes so they can drink some of their blood.

No one knew why Olivia's fangs never grew in.
She couldn't drink blood like the other children did.

She had to stick to eating lettuce, cheese, carrots,
cucumbers, bananas, oranges, strawberries, potatoes,
fish, hot dogs, chicken nuggets,
and ice cream sundaes
with hot fudge,
whipped cream,
pecan sprinkles
and a cherry on top.

Olivia hated her life.

Vampires have to sleep in their earth-filled coffins,
a box they usually put dead people in, as vampires can't
stand the sunshine.
Direct sunlight turns a vampire to ash within minutes,
so they must stay underground to sleep during the day,
and only come out at night when the sun goes away.

One day as Olivia was lying in her coffin, she began to wonder why the other kids could sleep so soundly during the day while she usually stayed wide awake.
She decided to do something she had never, ever done before.
She got out of her coffin and climbed the worn stone steps up to the front door of the castle.

She unbolted the door and carefully pushed it open a few inches on its ancient hinges. To her surprise, the bright sunlight that shone on her face felt warm and inviting and didn't turn her to ash at all.

Curious, she stepped outside
and closed the door behind her.

It was a wonderful Spring day. The grass lay lush and green all around, and birds chirped sweetly in the nearby forest. Puffy white clouds floated above in a sparkling blue sky, not at all the way they looked in the moonlight.

Olivia walked down the path that led to the village.

The people who lived there locked their doors and windows at night, as they were afraid of the vampires, but now they were walking about selling things and running errands without any fear.

Farmers worked their crops in the fields while children played in the alleys behind the shops.

The colors and smells were so wonderful
that Olivia thought she must be dreaming.

She remembered that all of the other vampires
would burn up if they came outside in the sunlight.

Why didn't she burn up?

She only felt a warm glow
as the sunlight tickled her skin.

Then a man in the village shouted,
and he pointed at Olivia.

"Look!" he cried. "That girl has come from the castle!"

Faster than you could eat an apple, the streets were deserted. Men, women and children were all inside their walls and window-shutters, and Olivia heard the "screech, thud" of bolts being locked tight.

Olivia felt bewildered as she stood alone
in the silent town, and wondered
what she should do next.

The vampire kids always made fun of her,
and now the humans hid themselves away.

She felt so lonely.

"Hello," a voice said behind her. She turned to see
a young couple standing there, dressed all in black.

"Hello," Olivia said hesitantly. "Who are you?"

"We saw the townspeople hide when they said you came from the castle," the man said. "Is that true?"

"Yes," Olivia said. "I live there."

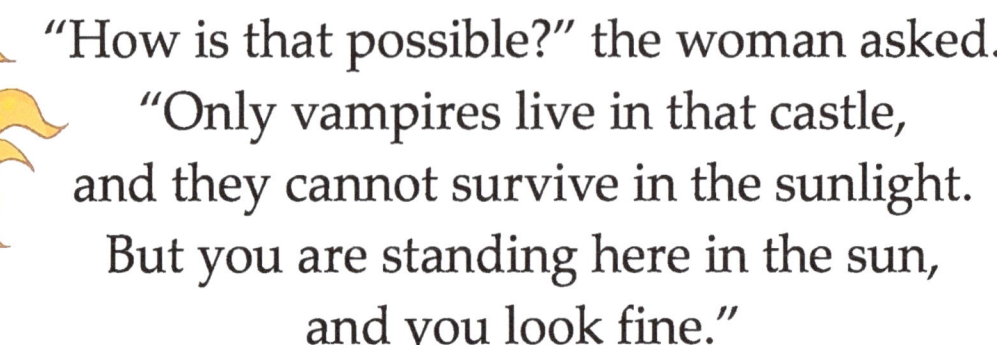

"How is that possible?" the woman asked.
"Only vampires live in that castle,
and they cannot survive in the sunlight.
But you are standing here in the sun,
and you look fine."

"I'm not fine," Olivia sighed. "I don't have any fangs like the other vampires." She bared her teeth so they could see.

The man bent down to look, and he sniffed the air with his great nose. His face broke into a smile, and he turned to the woman.

"Maria, it is her! I could never forget her scent!" He looked back at Olivia. "Seven years ago we were traveling through this region at night when we were attacked by vampires. We had to hide our baby daughter inside a hollow tree while we fought them, but when we came back, our girl was gone. We feared we would never see her again."

The woman nodded. "Tell me, dear girl, have you been living with the vampires your whole life?"

Olivia answered, "Yes, but I still don't understand. Why am I different from the other vampires?"

"Because you are not a vampire at all," the woman said.
You are our darling baby girl who disappeared
all those years ago during the battle.
The vampires must have adopted you.

But there is no denying it, you are our daughter.
Drago's sense of smell cannot be deceived."

"My name is Olivia," said Olivia.

"We had named you Sanya," the woman said.
"But you may decide which name you wish to use,
as you have had the other one for so long.

Please come and live with us!
We will love you and take care of you
as parents should."

Olivia felt tears run down her cheeks, tears of joy.
At last, she had found a place where she belonged.
"You're my parents? I'm not really a vampire?
And that's why I don't have fangs?"

She rushed to embrace them, and felt their loving arms
comfort her.

"Yes, my darling," her father said. "You are not a vampire, and that is why you have no fangs.
You are a werewolf like us, and when you get a little older the full moon will turn you into a shaggy wolf.

You will get your fangs then."

Duane Porter
is the author of eight books to date
and has received several awards
for children's literature.

Other books by Duane Porter:

The Best Ride

Charlie and the Chess Set
The Seirawan Factor

Molly O'Malley and the Leprechaun
Molly O'Malley: Rise of the Changeling
Molly O'Malley and the Pirate Queen

Werewolf for Hire: The Ghost of Goresthorpe Grange

www.ingramcontent.com/pod-product-compliance
Lightning Source LLC
Chambersburg PA
CBHW041541240626

47164CB00002B/87